My Dad and Me

by **Alyssa Satin Capucilli** • illustrated by **Susan Mitchell**

LITTLE SIMON

New York   London   Toronto   Sydney

When it's only my dad and me . . .

we rake the leaves high.

When it's only my *papi* and me . . .

Papi means "dad" in Spanish.

we spin as snow falls,

When it's only my *aba* and me . . .

Aba means "dad" in Hebrew.

we take morning hikes,

When it's only my *bàbà* and me . . .

Bàbà means "dad" in Mandarin.

we pick shells from the sand,

When it's only my *bapa* and me . . .

Bapa means "dad" in Hindi.

we celebrate every day,